FEATHER FALLS

GOLDEN STATE STORIES

SHAWN HARTJE

HELEN SPRINGS PRESS
SAN RAFAEL, CALIFORNIA

Copyright © 2024 by Shawn Hartje

All rights reserved. No part of this publication may be reproduced, distributed or transmitted in any form or by any means, including photocopying, recording, or other electronic or mechanical methods, without the prior written permission of the publisher, except in the case of brief quotations embodied in critical reviews and certain other noncommercial uses permitted by copyright law. For permission requests, write to the publisher, addressed "Attention: Permissions Coordinator," at the address below.

Shawn Hartje/Helen Springs Press
http://www.shawnhartje.com/

Publisher's Note: This is a work of fiction. Names, characters, places, and incidents are a product of the author's imagination. Locales and public names are sometimes used for atmospheric purposes. Any resemblance to actual people, living or dead, or to businesses, companies, events, institutions, or locales is completely coincidental.

Cover Photo by Jeremy Vesely http://www.jeremyvesely.com

Cover Design by ebooklaunch.com

Feather Falls, Golden State Stories/Shawn Hartje. - **1st print edition**

Contents

THE FEEDER 1

FEATHER FALLS 11

SOLAR MAXIMUM 2025 29

A NIGHT AT THE U-BALL 41

NOTE FROM THE AUTHOR 48

PIPELINER 49

THE FEEDER

Soothed by the heat and gurgling waves, Jackson wasted no time stripping off his clothes, guzzling a can of syrupy craft beer, eating a steak ciabatta sandwich, and then rolling onto a towel for a snooze. Ines grunted, already bored. They'd spent the morning viewing seal colonies in the state park, but she had a long to-do list for work, and there was no service at this secluded beach.

Early on in their relationship, Jackson being a nudist had complemented Ines's love of hiking and the outdoors. He'd acted like John Muir, marching her through Northern California's remarkable scenery, where his nudity seemed pure and came off as endearing activism. But gradually she learned that Jackson preferred staying close to parking lots. This way he could carry enough beer, delicacies, and fancy REI contraptions to make nature as comfortable as their living room. He was an expert at finding hideouts in heavily used parks where he could get naked and eat, drink and nap.

Jackson snored and burrowed into his towel. She pitched a beach umbrella across his sunburned ass and reflected he had much in common with the rotund Elephant Seals, which primarily fed and lounged on the sand. So he wasn't the trooper she'd thought, but he was easy to live with, and he had a knack for making her laugh.

Ines fidgeted and grew melancholic, something she had a knack for. When he awoke, she poked his hairy stomach and barked seal-like at him, which surprised her. Jackson pouted, rubbing his belly where it'd been poked. She fantasized they were seals living on the edge of the sea. Again she poked and barked at him. Jackson caught on that he was supposed to be a seal. Putting his bulk to work, he roared and flapped his arms like flippers, and the result was wonderfully accurate. Ines clapped, thrilled. Their clamorous barks echoed off the surrounding sea cliffs until neither of them could bark for laughing. Ines collapsed to the sand, half laughing and half barking. She was attempting to fend off a wave of melancholy, but it was short lived. From long experience, she recognized the onset of a severe depression. These spells had started in early childhood, in far away Kiruna, Sweden, north of the Arctic circle, and coincided with the Polar Nights of December and January when the sun never climbed above the horizon.

Jackson was also familiar with her spells and in a coup de grace he rolled onto his belly and slid toward the water in a seal-like fashion, driving his chest into the sand with his knees, his sunburned ass rising and falling like a worm. It was ridiculous and Ines thought she might love this goofy man, who seemed to be an antidote for her depression. Jackson was a produce manager at Whole Foods who had introduced himself to Ines with a corny joke in the aisles: *What's a chicken's favorite veggie? Bawk Choy!* Ines was suffering a bad spell at the time and nearly melted with gratitude. Her debilitating Polar Nights had yet to scare him away—but was this actually love?

Reaching the sea, Jackson turned to gauge her reaction and was compelled to enter the frigid water. With a bark he splashed into the ocean, diving under and resurfacing a good ways offshore with a piercing yelp. Energized, Jackson made a ruckus, barking and thrashing. The ocean erupted beneath him, rocketing him into the air. Beneath him followed a huge shark, its angular head bursting from the water, jaws agape. Flung high, Jackson twisted and rolled—somehow gracefully— and hit the water with a slap. He recovered quickly and floated with a stunned look on his face.

Horrified, Ines realized Jackson wasn't aware of the shark. Surely it would return and eviscerate him but it was gone as suddenly as it had come. Ines screamed, "Swim to me! Quickly!" Jackson looked around quizzically and started casually swimming to shore. How could he be such an idiot? He arrived on the beach and stood dripping wet while Ines examined him, and hugged him.

"You are fine! It's impossible you were not eaten!"

Jackson was awestruck when Ines told him a shark was responsible for the mayhem.

"What did you think happened?"

Jackson shrugged. "I dunno, babe. Like a mini tsunami? I didn't feel anything hit me, it was all water."

The couple studied the calm ocean in disbelief, waiting for something to happen. A cold fog swirled in, they dressed without speaking, and climbed out of the cove. They made their way through the brush to the established trail where Ines read a sign that she'd missed earlier. Leaving the trail had been illegal, the sign read—to protect the wildlife from visitors.

Ines drove back to San Francisco, steering with one hand and clasping Jackson's with the other. A peaceful giddiness settled over her, blocking her melancholy. The shark attack had been horrible to witness, but its otherworldliness was remarkable.

Jackson chattered manically about the event. "You know what the odds are for something like this? Cosmic forces were involved, a hundred-percent."

Ines hated this phrase, especially the way he enunciated "a hundred." He overused it, as did all of his friends. She pulled her hand free as he continued mansplaining. "I'm getting this weird freedom vibe. It's like everything and anything is possible. Crazy. Think I need a sando." He pulled another steak ciabatta from his well-stocked soft cooler behind the seat. "Dude," he said while chewing, "like I'm supposed to just go back to the veggie department?"

"Don't call me dude." Ines's irritability was a sign of her darkness, lurking sharklike beneath the adrenaline. Of course, Jackson sought meaning from the attack. He fully believed in cosmic forces while she thought the world was meaningless. This was largely due to her father's accidental death back when she was a teenager in Sweden. Her father, Koren, had charged into the snowy woods on his dogsled in pursuit of a hare and was ejected into deep snow. It was later determined that he'd survived the crash, but planting headfirst with his arms stuck fast had immobilized him. Ines imagined how desperately he must have kicked, to free himself and return to his family, buried alive and suffocating in the uncaring, meaningless snow of Lapland. Her little brother, Peter, coped with the accident by viewing it as glorious, while Ines fell into a prolonged Polar Night that never faded despite moving to sunny

California. Peter now lived in Alaska where he raced the famous Iditarod with a pluck that only his peculiar legacy could provide and which she resented. In Ines's mind, the risky behavior would catch up with him and she'd be forced to endure the family tragedy a second time.

Things were quiet that night in their San Francisco apartment. Jackson smoked weed, ate another sando, and listened to music on his headphones. Ines logged into work where she managed online advertising for an infant-supplies corporation. Each baby product had multiple ad campaigns running across various platforms. These needed frequent reviewing in order to boost performance and reap bonus pay—which she always did.

She finished working and studied Jackson, who nodded to the beat in his headphones. It irked her that he'd been right about the shark attack opening up possibilities. Despite dredging up painful memories from her father's accident, she felt a peaceful undercurrent stemming from the event. This was inexplicable and confusing.

She interrupted Jackson. "It's late. Come to bed with me?"

Jackson gave her a sideways look. "Sorry, babe. I'm all fired up tonight."

He was a night owl and usually stayed up late, strumming his guitar, drinking beer, and watching his favorite band 'Cosmic Twang' on Youtube. Tonight he was further energized by the shark attack and come morning she feared it would be impossible to put that genie back in the bottle. Indeed, Jackson called in sick the next morning. Then he turned on music and made pancakes.

"You're not sick," Ines said. "Stop being silly. Clean up your mess and go to work."

"I've got a ton of sick days to burn up."

"Why would you do that? What if you actually get sick?"

"That's not my present situation."

The present situation was untenable for Ines, who worked from their small apartment. Accustomed to having the place to herself, she fumed and cleaned up Jackson's beer cans and breakfast dishes while he strummed his guitar. He took a shower and tried on different Hawaiian shirts before choosing the loudest. When he finally sauntered out of the apartment, she looked at her morning reports. Diaper keywords were skyrocketing in price. A new competitor, DiaperWarehouseDirect, was bidding up the price, forcing her to pause all diaper ads; to compete at these rates would quickly drain her budget.

Jackson returned and videoed himself unpacking groceries and chopping veggies, narrating the process in a sing-songy fashion. "Lettuce make a salad! Red-leaf and BUTTERHEADED… Crunchy cucs and carrots gettin' SHREDDED!" Working smoothly, he'd soon whipped up an immense and beautiful salad, which he ate with his bare hands. He danced, chewing and pointing his oily fingers at his phone camera like toy guns. Ines was embarrassed for him. Why was he filming himself?

"Maybe you are sick? What is this?"

"I'm Vlogging, Babe. Gonna put myself out there."

Ines was aware of Jackson's dream of being famous and for this she blamed his mother. A law firm secretary in L.A., his mother had long dabbled in acting, never getting beyond small parts. She held onto grand aspirations for her only child, who, so far, hadn't made it beyond the so-called life of the party.

"Try using silverware," Ines said. "There's dressing all over that ridiculous shirt."

Jackson held up his hands in defense. "Sorry, Babe, but you gotta share me with the world."

"Shirking your duties and causing a ruckus when I have to work is nothing to share with the world. That stupid shark got into your head."

Jackson spoke thoughtfully, "You're the best thing that's ever happened to me, Babe. That's because I cook awesome stuff and make you laugh. I'm just going with what works."

Ines trembled beneath the surface, as if all she required was a good meal and a zippy joke.

"Don't be silly," she said. "You mean much more to me than laughs and flavorful meals."

Jackson didn't seem convinced. "If that's true, then you'll get behind me on this."

But she couldn't. She saw a child playing with a toy, a kid refusing to grow up. Whole Foods was considering him for regional produce buyer, but he hadn't followed up on it. She should ship him off for a month with brother Peter in Alaska. What actually happens when you refuse to grow up is that you freeze your ass off on a rickety dog sled.

As suspected, DiaperWarehouseDirect was well-funded and staffed with savvy digital marketers. Rather than caring about putting quality infant products in front of consumers, DiaperWarehouseDirect focused on gaming the online advertising ecosystem in order to disrupt the strategy of established infant care companies, the largest of which was Ines's employer. Not only was DiaperWarehouseDirect bidding up traditional keywords, they'd renamed an entire product category just to throw her off! Instead of bottles, they sold 'Feeders.' Feeders were trending in search queries and stealing market share while her company was hiring a consultant to determine if Feeders was an appropriate branding term. Her performance went down and she received no fourth quarter bonus pay. To make matters worse, Jackson used all his sick days to shoot his foodie Vlog. Then his supervisor found his YouTube channel and threatened to fire him.

Ines freaked out. "Do you care if you're fired?"

"She dug it, Babe. She subscribed to my channel!"

Ines explained how the Feeder debacle was screwing up her income, and they couldn't afford his behavior right now.

Jackson looked hurt. "These things take time. It'll happen for me. Thinking I might do a nude episode. I can blur out the beans and weenie, you know?"

"Seriously?"

"No, that was a joke. But you don't get my jokes anymore. What happened to us Babe?"

Ines said, "That shark happened. You were clueless. Only I saw how horrible it was." Her face buckled with emotion, and her normally subdued Swedish accent came on full-force. "That massive, ugly, deep-lurking FEEDER!"

Jackson said, "It didn't eat me. It came to test us."

"Enough of your cosmic blundering."

"I asked you to get behind me and you couldn't. If you really loved me, you'd support me no matter what. Have you even watched my episodes? I'm making you proud, Babe."

Feeling exposed, she fled to their bedroom and cried. The world had been plenty cruel to Ines. Her mother died when she was three, while giving birth to Peter. Losing her mother so young, followed by her father, had always been her excuse for chronic doom. But now she felt cursed by an evil predator of the deep, as if the Feeder had haunted her entire life. It had killed her parents, possessed her boyfriend and brother, and now it threatened her sanity.

Interrupting her spiral, brother Peter texted asking if she'd watched Jackson's latest episode. Being a risk taker, he'd been encouraging Jackson, which agitated her. She responded by asking how the dogsledding was going, already knowing from Jackson that he had a lame leader dog.

He replied, "Taking some time off. Dogs are expensive. Been substitute teaching at a high school."

What? She immediately called him for the details. The boys liked that he was a musher who hunted and trapped, and the girls liked his Swedish accent. She'd bitterly forced him to finish his degree in Sweden before heading to Alaska. She liked to think that he was putting his degree to use, and told him so.

Peter said, "The superintendent is a fellow musher. That's why he gave me the job. Nobody asked if I went to college."

He would never tire of convincing her that dogsledding was the answer to everything. She told him he sounded grown up, and asked if another young teacher had eyes for him. He asked if she would ever stop mothering him, and she said no.

Ines found Jackson's YouTube channel, Cosmic Grubs. Right off she didn't like the name. But talking to Peter had softened her heart, and she vowed to watch Jackson's videos with an open mind. He wore tacky Hawaiian shirts and prepared appetizing meals nonchalantly, while joking and singing. The episodes were named after dishes, like 'Eda-Mamma-Jamma,' an edamame and pork belly succotash. For such a large man, he sang in a comically high voice: *She's an Eda-Mamma-Jamma.* The most viewed episode was 'Twang Chowder,' featuring slow cooked brisket in a cream of celery broth. Here he sang a corny tale about a Beef-centric 49er from Texas who falls for a San Francisco fisherman's daughter: *and when he found her, they made Twang Chowder.* He ate a spoonful and daintily boogied. It was funny how his general bulkiness didn't undermine his grace as a dancer, and Ines caught herself laughing. She'd lost the sense of watching Jackson, and instead saw a guy who was genuinely funny without trying. She'd known he was funny, but never realized that he was a gifted comic. Briefly, she felt selfish about this and then was inspired by a voice in her head telling her to research domain names associated with Feeder. Using her own credit card, she bought them all, babyfeeder.com and feeder.com, among others. Then she made her company's products the landing pages for the new URLs. After a few days, traffic increased noticeably and so had sales.

But it had been too easy. The savvy gurus at DirectBabyWarehouse weren't likely to have missed something as crucial as owning the domain names before renaming a product category. From the get go, she'd suspected that these gurus were setting her up. A little online sleuthing determined that a VP at the equity firm behind DirectBabyWarehouse had also funded her company in the early days of the Dotcom boom. She messaged the guy on a networking app with the cryptic message: *let's talk*. She wasn't surprised to receive his nearly instant reply—*congrats on moving to the next round*. Guys like this didn't care about money, they were silly little boys who loved gamesmanship. This idiot could've just emailed her and offered her a job. Within a year she'd be running DirectBabyWarehouse, and he'd still be prowling for muscular sled dogs.

Jackson sat in his beer drinking chair, frowning at his phone.

Ines said, "I watched your videos."

"Yeah?"

"I laughed."

Jackson smiled, then frowned. "My subscriptions are flat. It's the name. Cosmic Grubs sounds like some disgusting hippie food truck."

"I think you should call it Feeder."

Jackson thought on this. "The Feeder?"

"Only Feeder."

"I like it. Okay!"

"I'm sorry I didn't get behind you. My depression is very blinding."

They had never openly discussed her depression before. She'd never admitted it to him, and assumed he thought she was just a severe person.

Jackson nodded. "When I first saw you in the produce section, I was attracted by your sadness."

"Really?"

"Seriously, Babe, I got special radar for sad people. That's because Mother Nature designed me to make people laugh. I also noticed how twanging hot you are!"

Ines broke down and sobbing was a great release. Though she never knew her mother, she felt close to her like never before. The shark flashed before her mind. She now saw what Jackson had known intuitively from the start, that the Feeder was from another dimension—a place where pure instinct gave no cause for depression.

Feather Falls

On a brushy slope above Lake Oroville, Ed Rushford pinned down a fat rattlesnake with a forked pole and then smashed its head with a boot stomp. He knew the types of logs and rocks to look under, having been wrangling snakes since he was a small boy. The snakeskin might fetch forty bucks at the highway pullout where his father, Cal Rushford, also sold firewood, bear jerky, and Republic of California flags from his truck's tailgate. Losing interest in snake hunting, Ed peered through his rifle's scope at an elaborate houseboat that had anchored in a narrow reservoir inlet. Surrounding the boat and floating on rafts were the loveliest girls Ed had ever seen.

"What ya looking at?" his father said, sneaking up on him.

Ed jumped back from the scope as Cal laughed at him. Cal pulled a knife off his belt loop and expertly split the snake's belly and fingered out its insides. The entrails landed in a bloody pile, half on his boots.

"I'll be making for the truck," Cal said. "Follow up when you's done peeping."

Cal loped up to the ridge, the snake corpse swinging from his hand. Ed stared at the fly covered snake guts for a moment and then went back to looking at the girls. He was the type of teenaged boy who couldn't stand being around girls because they overwhelmed him. He didn't get any pleasure from viewing these girls, but he couldn't stop staring. He prayed for the strength to look away. A horsefly bit him and he jerked away from the scope—the Lord provides!

Lugging his gear up the mountain, the hot sun was killing him. Save for his ball cap, he was ill-dressed for the triple digit heat with his canvas pants, tall leather boots, and a plaid, snap-button shirt. If he stood in direct sunlight, the metal buttons would scald his chest. Since the brushy woods were thick with poison oak, ticks, and rattlers, he dressed like a woodsman, just like his father did. Few men in their mountain enclave of Feather Falls went around like lumberjacks in the superheated summers, let alone at all. It was dawning on young Ed just how much of a character his father was.

He found Cal perched on the tailgate of his Chevy drinking a beer, scrutinizing their haul of rattlesnakes. Ed rode silently in the truck, wondering if girls were an entirely different species than him. It was heartbreaking to think that he wasn't compatible with girls, but this explained why he couldn't communicate or deal with them in any way. He eyed Cal at the steering wheel, whose unkempt hair flapped in the warm breeze flowing through the windows. Cal seemed at ease with the world, steering lazily with one hand, the other holding a can of beer and a tiny cigar. Cal frequented the large casino near Oroville, often with Ed in tow, who noticed how his father's mischievous smile and handlebar mustache caught the attention of certain waitresses and other women with whom he seemed to be familiar. Ed supposed he could learn something from his father about girls.

In Feather Falls, Cal stopped at the tiny market for beer, bratwurst, and cheap cigars and then drove up the mountain through the burn scar of last year's massive fire. Nothing had survived the mega fire. Even the most stately pines had been scorched black and now stood like sentinels of disease. The smaller trees that hadn't been vaporized were haphazardly collapsed into treacherous tangles, making the burn scar a no-man's-land. Ed still wasn't used to the transformation from green to black, especially how the sky and distant topography had become visible. Having lived on the mountain his whole life, it was nothing short of a mind warp. They crested a rocky rise where the fire had stopped. The green forest returned, the temperature dropped, and the air once again smelled like pine sap and white granite. The smell of Sierra granite was peculiar and Ed likened it to something ancient.

They turned onto their driveway where Ed unlocked a heavily paddle-locked gate. Fake surveillance cameras conspicuously pointed at the gate. No trespassing signs warned of armed response, but these, Ed knew, weren't bluffs. Once through the gate, the forest thinned due to granite outcrops and Bald Rock Canyon of the Middle Feather River was visible below. This canyon was inaccessible from here as sheer granite walls dropped thousands of feet into the river chasm. The property was an inholding within the Plumas National Forest. According to Cal, it had been settled in the early 19th century by his long-ago great great grandfather, who as a Californio, predated the 49ers. It had been a worthless mining claim, as the gold was found in the low terrain along the gravel bars in the river canyon. But the prolific spring that gushed forth between granite boulders was better than gold, as Cal claimed the mineral content of its water reversed the aging process. He was fifty five, a daily drinker and smoker, and ran around the mountains with the energy of a twenty-year old. Indisputable, however, was that the unlimited water supply, sunny climate, and remote location allowed Cal to easily grow marijuana.

Ed's home life was filled with chores, especially concerning firewood. Reaching the pair of fifth-wheel trailers they called home, Ed went straight to the woodpile and split logs for an hour, then stacked wood for another hour. Freshly cut pine took two years to cure, and Ed knew the timeline of each stack by heart. He loaded the pickup bed with cured wood, which tomorrow they would sell to campers headed into the mountains. Next he went and fed the bear dogs, a friendly group of Coonhounds and Catahoulas. Only by diverting the beasts with kibble, could he clean their kennel. Otherwise the energetic pack would never leave him alone, jumping and begging to play. He'd learned to not get attached, as the dogs were somewhat disposable. It wasn't that they were abused, but they frequently didn't return to the truck after chasing bears, and God only knew how they ended up. Finally, he fleshed the snakeskins with a spoon, and washed them in the creek.

He showered in his own trailer and sat in the air conditioning. He used to live with his father in the sprawling cabin near the spring, but since the big fire, Cal—ever adaptable to life in the woods—had moved them into the trailers. In the event of another fire, he could just tow them out of the way. But the night the mega fire broke out, Cal had been at the casino and Ed was alone on the mountain. He remembered that night was unusually humid with thunderstorms surrounding the property. Lightning flashed, but no rain fell. He smelled smoke, watched ash fall like snowflakes, and then it became difficult to breath. The fire consumed the far rim of the canyon, the flames crowning high above the tall trees. Watching the sky turn blood orange, Ed thought of the many snakes he'd killed, none of which had turned away from their deaths. But how would he face this fire? He prayed for strength to face what he knew would be an agonizing death. He brought the spooked dogs to the spring where they huddled instinctively near the water. Ed wet his shirt and breathed through the wet fabric, surprised to find his mind turning clear as the spring water. It was a miracle the property hadn't burned. It was now an island amidst 300,000 acres of scorched earth. Cal thought it had something to do with the spring, but Ed believed that the Lord worked mysteriously.

In any case, Ed preferred his new trailer to the ratty old cabin. The trailer had all the amenities of a modern home. The only personal effect was a large snakeskin mounted on a stained board hanging above the dining booth. On his father's suggestion, Ed had wood-burned the phrase, "Don't Tread On Me" below the skin. This was the only snake to ever bite Ed, who'd clumsily dropped his snare pole mid capture. The strike lacked the momentum to fully pierce his leather boots and only a small amount of venom entered through the wound on his foot. The resulting fever was minimal and had been a strangely pleasant experience. Maybe it was because he had an excuse to lay around, or maybe he had a peculiar sensitivity to rattlesnake venom. Whatever the cause, Ed fondly remembered the experience as dreamy.

Cal grilled the bratwursts and they ate at the picnic table between the trailers, watching the sun fade over the immense canyon. In the morning, Ed removed the older, treated snakeskins from their stretching racks and pinned out the new ones. In the cabin, he loaded bear jerky and ice from the deep freeze into a massive cooler along with mason jars of spring water. Packed with inventory they headed down the mountain to Cal's strategic pullout high above the reservoir. Here they drew campers going into the national forest, and also boaters headed to the marinas and boat ramps of Lake Oroville.

Cal set himself in an antique rocking chair under a pop up tent, puffing tiny cigars and crossing his long legs, his scuffed boots jutting out like stumps. Strung from the tent and flapping in the hot breeze were iconic Bear Republic flags, featuring a lone Grizzly Bear and a singular red star.

A suburban towing a speedboat pulled over and out climbed a smiling, paunchy dad followed by a pretty mom and two boys. The dad wasn't shy, pointing rudely at Cal, "It's the bear jerky guy! Hey man, can I get a photo?"

Cal posed agreeably while Ed fetched jerky from the cooler, inserting a fact sheet on the Bear Flag Revolt into the ziplock. The man fumbled on his phone, "Can I Venmo you?"

Cal shook his head. "Horses, guns, or ammo are the preferred payments, but I also take cash." The wife dug a twenty from her purse and handed it to Cal. "Preciate that ma'am." He made full eye contact and tipped his head at her. Ed noticed that her attitude went from boredom to interest. Cal coaxed their two young boys into opening a cigar box on the table filled with rattlesnake rattles. The big ones, he said, were from Western Diamondbacks and the small ones were Northern Pacific Rattlers. "Wanna know which one's the meanest?"

The open-mouthed boys nodded.

"Whichever one you's trying to catch!" Cal laughed good-heartedly. The mom also laughed and when Cal handed her a five dollar bill in change he managed to squeeze her hand affectionately. Shockingly, she didn't appear to mind. Ed watched for the husband to notice this flirting, but he was also sifting open-mouthed through the rattles.

"Say boys," Cal said, "Did they teach the Bear Flag Revolt in your school?"

The boys shrugged, staring open-mouthed as Cal told his favorite story.

"You surely know about the American Revolution. Well, in 1846, California had its own revolution. A group of mountain men called the Californios overthrew the Mexican Government, declaring independence for California. But a month later, the American military marched in and claimed it for itself! But by God this beautiful place we live in was meant to be free. There were more Native Americans living here than anywhere, and they lived freer than any people to ever walk the earth! The Californios fought with the Tribes and competed for the same resources, but this was a fair fight. Now The Californios and the Tribes together could've chased out the Missionaries, but the American Government was a hungry beast, and no amount of land or taxes could ever fill 'er up. Once gold was found, it was game over for independence. Gold fever engorged the beast and brought out the worst in just about everyone. The honorable story of the Californios and the Tribes got buried beneath 49er lore, but I reckon there's still a few holdouts. Those genes die hard."

Cal winked at the boys, and then gave eyes to their mom, who was no dummy. She said, "You're an excellent story-teller. You know I teach fourth grade? I'd invite you to visit my class, but your story's inaccurate. The Bear Flaggers were happy for American help."

Cal was no stranger to rebukes. "History is written by the victors. But you're in luck, because each purchase comes with an informational pamphlet written by yours truly. You may doubt what happened, but I will tell you for a fact, ma'am, that the Bear Revolt is ongoing!"

Ed had heard his father's spiel countless times, but this exchange was charged by the woman's obvious attraction to Cal. Usually when teachers encountered his father, the result was an outpouring of sympathy to Ed. Clearly this woman was a risk taker, and Ed filed this away for later use.

"Now boys," Cal said, "Take a rattle on the house today. That goes for you too, sir."

The husband raised his eyebrows, thanking Cal.

"And keep your eyes on the forest," Cal continued, "It's rumored there might be a few Grizzlies left way back up that Feather River."

When the family drove off, Cal said, "Nice woman, stupid family."

Sales slowed into the evening and Ed broke down the makeshift store. Cal counted the proceeds but didn't share. Ed didn't mind, he was seeing his mother this weekend, and she'd send him home flush. He met her in the Gold Country Casino parking lot—once Cal had gone inside.

"How's Cal," his mother asked.

"Same, I suppose."

"For a man who doesn't gamble, he sure loves this casino."

"He likes the bar. He knows everyone."

Ed was uncomfortable discussing Cal with his mom. It was out of character for her to right-off ask about Cal. She either sensed something, or more likely had heard something. Her family worked in the casino and kept their ears to the ground.

"Let me know if he starts getting cagey on you. You can come live with us again."

"He's always been cagey."

"Anyone new been around the property?"

"I don't think so."

Ed hated discussing his living arrangements. When his parents had first separated, Ed moved to Chico with his mom, Beverly, who'd sought a fresh start away from her family. They were Tribal Maidus, and the money pouring in from the casino had divided them. Ed thought his mom looked white, and she certainly had a white woman's life, but her mother—Ed's grandmother—looked like what he considered a Maidu looked like. Ed thought it strange how he looked like his Maidu grandmother, and also Cal, but not his mom.

They drove the thirty minutes to Chico, and picked up pizzas from a crowded place, full of well-off women who all seemed to know Beverly. Ed shouldn't have been surprised by this, but he was still getting used to his mom's life. Chico was a town full of trees, and Beverly's neighborhood had the oldest, most beautiful trees in town. Sitting around their spacious dining room table, Ed ate delicious pizza with his mom's husband Kyle, and his kids, Mark and Renee. He was familiar enough with everyone to not be totally uncomfortable, having briefly lived here with them, but he was far from relaxed.

Kyle asked Ed how his summer was going, but failed to jumpstart a conversation. Renee and Mark looked at their phones, clearly feeling as awkward as Ed.

It grew uncomfortable enough that Ed prayed for something to say, "I love my new trailer. It's got a microwave, fridge, and air conditioning. There's a satellite for TV and internet, but I haven't got the subscription. We lost two dogs this summer, one chasing bear, and I think the neighbor down the road shot the other."

"Is that right?" Kyle asked. Kyle was a farmer, more specifically he managed his family's extensive orchards in the Sacramento River Valley. He'd always been kind and welcoming to Ed, but Ed never felt at home in Kyle's big house. Mark said he was going out with friends, and asked if Ed would like to join him. Clearly, Kyle or Beverly had put Mark up to this, and Ed was mortified. He found the strength to politely decline, said he was tired.

Mark said, "good seeing you man," and made a quick exit. Renee usually ignored him, but tonight she gave him a knowing smile before leaving and Ed couldn't breathe for nearly a minute. What was she thinking about him?

Kyle went to bed early, and Ed watched TV with Beverly, feeling strange. Something had changed in his world. He remembered the girls from the houseboat. Renee would fit in with those girls, and for some reason she'd checked him out. Renee was pretty, but he wasn't thinking about her in that way. He couldn't shake feeling that her look had something to do with his life on the mountain, as if it held secrets that only he could know.

Beverly asked if he'd go to church with her and Kyle on Sunday. They were "big-time" Christians, as Cal said. Ed's mom had brought him up Christian, but since the fire, God had ceased being a distant figurehead and become something far more intimate.

Ed asked if Mark and Renee were going.

Beverly shook her head. "I know it's hard for you with them."

Ed said he looked forward to going, and hoped it wouldn't end up with her begging him to come live here. It had been painful living with them the first time because he'd felt so different from everyone else. He couldn't imagine returning. His mom went to bed and he watched YouTube on their big TV, which fed him endless videos of people doing amazing feats, and he found it boring to watch so much of it.

Renee walked into the kitchen. "Hi Ed."

Ed got up to leave.

"Wanna beer?" she said.

Ed froze.

"You hardly say anything. I'm having one, don't tell, okay?"

Ed nodded.

Renee sat on the couch, patting the spot next to her. Ed sat down. He couldn't believe it, but he relaxed and listened to Renee ramble about her night. She finished her beer quickly. "Think I should have another one?"

Obviously she was a risk taker. There was an opportunity to take advantage of her daring—being her step-brother and being mysterious gave him an edge. Who was having these thoughts? He'd never considered himself mysterious or opportunistic before. He remained calm, while she twirled her hair and waited for him to kiss her.

Finally she said, "Dude, are we going to make out or what?"

Of course he wanted to kiss her. She was lovely in every way. But more thrilling was that he didn't feel the urge to turn away or freeze. He had amazing control over himself. Desire burned within his body, but his mind was pure spring water. Renee turned pale and looked like she'd made a mistake. She ran upstairs without another word.

At church on Sunday, Ed sat between Kyle and Beverly, wearing new clothes Beverly had bought him. The sermon concerned the 'Rich Young Ruler' parable from the book of Matthew, where Jesus tells a rich guy to give away his wealth and possessions in order to reach heaven. Kyle squirmed throughout before tossing a thick wad of bills onto the collection plate. Ed thought about his new trailer. He planned to hang his new clothes in its sleek closet and wear them to school that fall. These possessions made him happy and it'd be stupid to give away what the Lord had provided. But he understood what Jesus meant. When the mega fire had raged on the mountain, and it appeared that everything he knew was going to be lost, he was completely fine and peaceful.

After church they went to a nice steakhouse on a highway outside of town. Mark and Renee met them here, and Renee was back to ignoring him. Kyle and Beverly greeted many other families, whom Ed supposed were also rich farmers. Before eating, Beverly prayed, saying she was thankful that Ed had gone to church with her. Kyle was thankful for everyone's health and for a spectacular growing season. Mark and Renee looked annoyed and kept quiet. Beverly waited for Ed to give thanks. Previously this would've paralyzed him, but he immediately spoke.

"I don't need to pray anymore for strength. I'm already as strong as I could ever be."

The rest of the family exchanged confused looks, though Renee made eye contact with him. It appeared that she understood him.

"Honey," Beverly said, "I think you mean you're thankful that God has provided you with a strong faith."

Ed didn't see any difference. He still felt totally different from these people, only now it was clear that he was more advanced than them.

Beverly drove him back to Oroville that night, talking strangely about her mother. "I grew up thinking my mother knew secrets, you know, like real Indian medicine. But she never shared anything with me. She hardly talked to us. My youngest brother goes around acting like a shaman."

Ed considered that Beverly went around acting like a rich white woman. But she *was* a rich white woman, despite being part Maidu. He knew her extended family fought over what it meant to be Maidu. This had involved genetic testing, casino profit sharing, and positions with the gaming corporation. But his mom was hinting that there was a spiritual side to her family that was either secretive or had been lost beneath the quarreling.

Beverly sighed. "Spiritual pride is still pride, honey. Don't go around thinking you're something that you're not."

When school started Beverly and Kyle bought Ed a new pickup truck and a smartphone. Now he could communicate with the wider world and drive himself down the mountain to school. Previously, he'd taken the bus from Feather Falls, or depended on Cal for rides. They also didn't want him stranded on the mountain if another fire blew through. Everyone was increasingly paranoid about fire, while Ed grew less concerned about it. In fact, the mega burn scar started feeling normal to him. An early rainstorm came in October, easing fire concerns. He and Cal ventured cautiously into the burn scar to pick wild mushrooms, which thrived amongst the charred logs. Butte County started hassling Cal over selling roadside jerky, and now wild mushrooms, without a food permit. Cal's response was to print pamphlets actively calling for a modern day Bear Revolt. People came to the pullout not so much for merchandise, but rather for impassioned, anti-government rhetoric. Ed was shocked by all the people—men and women—who came to listen to Cal. Just as Beverly had warned, strange men began showing up on the property. Ed suspected they had something to do with Cal's pot business, but snooping around the property, Ed couldn't find anything from the grows. Cal had never hid it that well, and so he'd clearly been determined to get rid of the evidence.

Ed's grandma died in November. He hadn't seen his grandma in years, and had never been close with her. His mom's family held a traditional ceremony at a riverside park along the Feather River. Ed came with Cal, who knew Beverly's family far better than Kyle did, who squirmed throughout the ceremony. Clearly, much thought had gone into the ceremony. His mom's youngest, and supposedly shamanic, brother lead the chants and blessings, the gist of which said they were part of something greater, and to which Ed nodded his agreement. Nobody danced around fires, or wore traditional clothes, which Ed half expected. From his uncle's speech, Ed got the sense that his grandma had been difficult to live with. "She never spoke. We never knew what she wanted. This made us better people."

Afterward they gathered in a banquet hall at the Gold Country Casino where Beverly had set up photos from her mother's life. Ed saw photos of his grandfather, who'd died before Ed was born. He looked like the men from the nice steakhouse where Kyle and Beverly knew everyone. This was what his uncles looked like. But his grandma looked like him. His grandma died in her sleep, and Ed sensed that she'd already faced her death long before it came for her body. This was a strange thought, and he questioned who exactly was thinking this.

There was a buffet dinner and people tried to lure Ed into conversation which he deflected with one or two word responses. He wasn't trying to be reticent—it came naturally. The real wonder was how it'd ceased making him uncomfortable. In fact people liked being around him now, something he'd also noticed at high school. Once people realized they couldn't get him talking, they ignored him, while staying in close proximity. Ed was so close to God, that he needn't hanker for much of anything, and he believed people were attracted to this.

Kyle appeared to relax while eating with Beverly's oldest brother, whose connections to the casino and tribe meant he ran in the same circles as Kyle. They commiserated over Butte County's lack of cheap housing for both farmworkers and casino employees. Alcohol wasn't served at the dinner, although Cal was on his home turf, and managed to have a beer in hand, while inviting his friends from the casino bar to crash the buffet. It seemed that he managed this without offending anyone because nobody expected anything else from him. Ed's uncles, who'd known Cal their whole lives, seemed pleased to catch up with him. Even Kyle looked entertained by Cal. Beverly was the only one avoiding Cal, sitting apart with other guests, while keeping an eye on her ex-husband.

The talk turned to Cal's social media presence. Snippets from his roadside lectures had been circulating online. Cal didn't use the internet, but the new characters Ed had seen at the pullout and around the property certainly did. Cal laughed at the mention of his expanded notoriety. Ed's Shaman Uncle asked Cal half-jokingly if he was really planning a present day Bear Revolt against the government. Cal scratched his whiskered chin and said, "People do get carried away."

When pressed on which government he planned to overthrow—state or federal—he shrugged. "The problem ain't so much with the sows, it's with all them little piggies."

Ed's Casino Uncle gestured behind him toward the casino floor. "Those little piggies spread it around though."

This brought chuckles, especially from Cal "That's the beautiful thing about America. Everybody has the right to be stupid."

That night, Ed lay in his trailer quivering with energy. The large dose of family had turbocharged his thoughts. He sensed his uncles agreed with Cal's anti-government sentiments. Maybe this was a Maidu thing, a deep-seated hate passed down from ancestors. But since his uncles lived in abundance, he felt sorry for them. If they were close to God, like he was, they wouldn't want for anything. Looking out over Bald Rock Canyon, the granite glowed fluorescent in the moonlight. How lucky he was to live in such a powerful place. But would he remain strong if this were taken away from him? A shiver ran up his spine, and his mother's warning about pride came to mind. Suddenly, living in busy Chico, amongst the strip malls and wide boulevards, seemed to be his greatest fear.

In January, a tourist from the Bay Area filmed Cal driving across a bridge over the Feather River with his alpha bear dog, Bowser, chained to the hood of his truck. The filmer waved him down and accused him of animal cruelty. She returned home and posted the full encounter, which circulated widely due to Cal's growing internet fame.

"Sir, why is your dog chained to the hood of your truck?"

Cal smirked, "So he don't fall off."

"Do you think it's okay to chain your dog like that?"

"He likes it up there."

The woman panned to Bowser, feet spread wide on a patch of astroturf, straining his neck against the chain that was bolted to the hood.

"He seems incredibly anxious."

"Correct," Cal said. "He's anxious to chase a bear."

Bowser rode the hood to better scan for bear scent, and would eagerly jump onto this perch without any coaxing. But Cal didn't explain any of this.

"Lady, I'm confused. You're feeling sorry for Bowser?"

"Yes. This is barbaric, and I hope it's illegal!"

Cal scratched his beard, smiling. "You oughta feel sorry for the bear. Once the dogs tree 'em, I harvest them with my sidearm here." He casually pulled a handgun from under the seat, ejecting the clip for show. "The bigger ones'll take a full clip, bawlin' the whole way down."

"You…! I'm reporting you!"

Cal laughed and drove off honking his horn, which started Bowser howling on his chain. Watching the video, Ed couldn't remember his dad offending anyone like this. Every kind of person had stopped at the pullout over the years, and nobody had taken Cal seriously. The video's circulation subsided and was mostly forgotten except for in Butte County, where Cal became a sensation. The attention followed Ed to school, which made people even more curious about him. In English class, a girl named Gloria started sitting next to him, studying him.

"Is your dad starting a war?" she asked.

Ed shrugged. He was convinced that Gloria was one of the girls he'd seen floating near the houseboat, through the rifle scope.

Gloria said, "I never noticed you until this year. Did you go to another school or something?"

Ed shook his head.

"Everyone says you're impossible to talk to. Are you keeping secrets?"

Gloria slowly twirled her pencil in her long black hair, her dark eyes fluidly taking everything in. Her skin was brown and soft-looking and her movements precise and graceful. For someone who was so inviting, she was incredibly direct with him.

"I'm parked by the gym. Look for me after school. I promise you, Ed, I can handle your secrets."

Gloria drove a shiny-orange Dodge Charger. The car was loud and she wasn't afraid to rev the engine, racing along the network of levee roads along the main stem Feather River south of Oroville.

"Why the silence, Ed?"

Ed prayed for the right words. "Um, it's just my nature."

"Is that your secret?"

"Kinda."

Gloria parked in a wide pullout. The river here was broad and slow, flowing muddy through the orchards and rice paddies. Ed also felt sluggish and prayed for the the clarity of the headwaters. He was ashamed for reverting to prayer, but the coolness he'd experienced with Renee had abandoned him.

"I got a secret for you, Ed. I didn't talk until I was seven. My parents kept me out of school, thought I was autistic. I guess it took me that long to figure out what to say."

Ed confided. "I don't speak much because I don't like the noise. Even when I think, it's quiet, like hearing sounds from another room."

Gloria grabbed his hand and it was like being shocked. "Am I being too loud, Ed? I'd better shut up then."

She pulled the hair from her face, leaned over and kissed him. He fell into a void. She seemed to contain every possibility the world had ever known. Returning to earth, Ed felt dreamy—much like when he'd been snakebit.

Gloria dropped him at his truck and as she roared down the parking lot, he got chills noticing the sticker of the iconic coiled snake on her rear windshield, "Don't Tread On Me." After this, Ed began noticing these stickers around school and town. In the stealth of night, a prankster raised a "Don't Tread On Me" flag on the high school flagpole. The school held an assembly where Ed learned that the coiled snake flag was called the Gadsden flag, and it was offensive to Native Americans and people of color due to its association with the American Revolution and colonization. But the assembly didn't go as planned for the school officials. It turned out that the students—the majority of whom weren't white—overwhelmingly supported overthrowing the government. Gloria was the loudest, shouting at the principal, "*WE* don't need you mansplaining some woke-ass story about this flag. This flag represents oppressed people and you're just scared because brown people are flying it!"

The assembly hall erupted with cheers from the students. The Sheriff's deputies that were lined up behind the administration began to squirm, reminding Ed of Kyle. After the assembly, Bear Revolt and Gadsden Flag stickers adorned every locker, especially among students of color. Gloria caught Ed at his locker, questioning him about his ethnicity and demanding an introduction to Cal. "Are you gonna stay quiet, Ed?"

Gloria looked stunning in a snug-fitting, tie-dye Bear Revolt tank-top and yoga pants. Largely due to Gloria, Ed was back to praying on a daily basis.

"I don't see it like you," he said.

"They're calling your father a racist."

Indeed, the reactions to Cal's videos were flooded with racist supporters, as if the Bear Revolt was entirely a movement of angry white men.

Gloria said, "If you don't speak up Ed, they're gonna control the narrative. Are you ashamed of your ancestors, Ed?"

Ed prayed for understanding. "Pride is pride."

"Your ancestors resisted. Why don't you?"

To Ed, the coiled snake didn't symbolize politics or race. It was far more expansive. It was his birth and his death, and his desire for Gloria—which was creation itself.

Ed repeated, "I don't see it like you."

"How do you see it, Ed?"

The words suddenly came to him, "You feel the earthquake, but I am the cause."

The ground shook, the walls trembled, and they held each other. After the tremor passed, Ed saw that Gloria was just as scared as he was. Ed later felt tricked. Being close to God wasn't turning out the way he'd expected.

Gloria gossiped about Ed's earthquake premonition and this supercharged the Bear Revolt. Mother nature had spoken up in support, and the movement became tinged with religious fervor. Ed stopped going to school, as people treated him like a messiah, but it wasn't much better on the mountain. Cal was cautious around him, God only knew what rumors had reached him. Truckloads of supporters poured into Feather Falls, where the market flew Gadsden and Bear Revolt flags, while using the Stars and Stripes as a doormat.

People camped out on the property and Ed was shocked by the amount of trash piling up. Even Cal seemed caught off-guard by the momentum and as a result stayed drunk. But Ed suspected he was up to something and creeped on him to figure it out.

Cal's inner circle consisted of two men who'd taken residency in the cabin. They never left the cabin and only Cal visited them. Cal was leaving the cabin carrying a heavy duffel bag when Ed approached him by the spring.

Ed said, "You starting a war, dad?"

"No."

"What's in the bag?"

"Bear Revolt souvenirs."

Ed understood. "Guns?"

Cal winked, but seemed embarrassed, as if he'd let Ed down. "Come on, boy. It's just an act."

"Then why are you scared?"

Cal flinched briefly and then marched off. The creek leaving the spring was silty from all the people coming and going. The surrounding ferns were littered with excrement and toilet paper. It was heartbreaking. But the day grew worse when Kyle and Beverly showed up. Kyle stood near his truck, squirming, while Beverly had a private discussion with Cal.

Beverly returned alone and told Ed he had to leave the mountain.

"I'm sorry for skipping school," he said.

Kyle and Beverly shook their heads. Skipping school was the least of his problems. They said federal agents were in town, openly telling people they were going to shut down the Bear Revolt—the easy way, or the hard way.

Ed feared for his father. "Did you warn dad?"

"He knows," Beverly said, breaking into tears.

Kyle stepped in. "We've talked to these agents, Ed, they don't want trouble. That's why they're doing public relations. Everybody knows the score, none of these men up here really want to fight the United States."

Ed nodded. "It's all an act."

Ed gathered his clothes from his trailer, and then watched the sun set over the canyon. The mega fire, the spring, the smell of granite and pine sap, the ever-present roar from Bald Rock Canyon, the bear dogs and now Gloria—it was heartbreaking to lose it all. He studied the mounted "Don't Tread On Me" snakeskin and felt a fight brewing in him. If life as he knew it wasn't worth fighting for, then what was?

His mother found him crying, holding the mounted snakeskin. She took it carefully from him and left it in the trailer, leading him outside. He said goodbye to the dogs, and then stopped at the spring, where his father joined him. Ed said goodbye and Cal responded with a huge shrug, clearly an admission that indeed he was scared. Walking away from life on the mountain, Ed had never been closer to God.

Solar Maximum 2025

Penny, a lumpy Labrador, stretches on the sunny driveway. Joe the dog trainer places a shock-collar around her neck. This is no ordinary training collar. Using a key, Joe secures the locking chain around Penny's neck and winks at Helen, the dog's owner. Joe developed these elaborate shock collars during a career handling exotic animals—raising bears, wolves, and mountain lions in captivity for Hollywood productions. Using electricity to control those animals wasn't his preferred method, but it had saved his ass more than once. Demand for "Joe's Hot Chains" has surpassed all expectations, which he credits to a joke marketing slogan on his website: *inescapable by any animal, including children!*

Joe tells the owner, "Look how I got it snug against her skin? See how the probes on the individual links penetrate the fur? Otherwise, she won't feel any shock."

Penny rolls onto her back, inviting Joe to scratch her belly. Joe obliges and Penny groans with delight.

"I'm so glad I found you," Helen says. "Penny is so aggressive with other dogs, and her barking is maddening. Please understand she really is a pest."

Joe understands. He passes the remote control for the Hot Chain to Helen. She grips it like a pistol and curls her finger over the button.

An attorney friend recommended that Joe bill himself as a dog trainer and only provide this equipment after a pricy in-home consultation, so he can ensure there's an ornery pet in need of serious behavioral adjustments.

Joe says, "Try a firm command and leash correction before giving a shock. Be consistent. Only deliver a shock for insubordination."

Helen studies the control dials. "Will the level of shock be sufficient?"

"There's a weight chart to set the shock level. The highest level will stun a 300-pound-bear, so you can imagine what that would be like for a sixty pound dog."

"Right." Helen licks her lips. "But were I to accidentally zap her with the high setting, it wouldn't kill her?"

"Nah. The voltage is too low for that. But the current on the high setting, well, I wouldn't recommend it for anyone, er, I mean dog."

"Good." Helen again flexes her hand on the remote.

Joe's eager to collect payment and split. Helen's intensity has him feeling creepier than normal.

Helen hands over a credit card. "I need two. The extra one I'll keep at our Tahoe house. One less thing to pack."

Joe says to call if she needs help, reminding himself to block her number.

Helen removes the Hot Chain from Penny, who's fallen asleep in full belly rub posture, and goes inside to prepare. She hopes the kids won't find chicken soup odd on a hot day, but then it's a favorite dish. With the soup on a low simmer, she plugs in the Hot Chains to make sure they're fully charged.

Her security camera network alerts her phone. It's Billy, her fifteen year old son. On her gate camera she watches him doing wheelies—helmet-less—down the bustling highway. He's riding his friend Sam's so-called e-bike, which is really a full fledged motorcycle that goes 70mph and which Billy is forbidden to ride. Billy hops off and fist-bumps Sam and the two of them hit their vape pens. It's their afternoon ritual and Helen's seen it before.

Billy enters the kitchen and she confronts him about riding Sam's motorcycle and getting high. Knowing that she obsessively watches her camera network, he doesn't deny it. "Oh my fucking god, will you shut up! It's not a motorcycle. It has pedals. We know what we're doing!"

Helen says, "It's got a motor and a throttle, which makes it a motorcycle. You're getting high and riding motorcycles in an extreme fashion. I can't think of anything riskier."

Billy says, "What are you gonna do about it? Install more cameras to spy on me? You've been up in my business for so long, I'm immune to it. Do you honestly think I give a shit anymore?"

Locking horns with Billy is futile. Grounding him, confiscating his phone, or handing out any form of punishment would only further enrage him. Helen reminds herself that Billy is forcing her to take extreme measures. But first, she calls Sam's mother and gives her an earful. How can you allow your son to zip around Napa Valley on a dangerous, illegal machine, cutting through intersections, vineyards, schoolyards, and parking lots at ridiculously high speeds, performing wheelies and other stunts, blatantly disregarding traffic laws, having no driver's license or helmet—and did you know he's also stoned?

Sam's mother says, "What are you going to do about it?"

Helen is recording the conversation and responds accordingly. "Since law enforcement is failing to act, I have no recourse."

"So you're the one who ratted my son to the cops?"

Helen had done just that, but acts shocked.

"I would never! I am merely concerned that society is failing to protect our children."

"I feel sorry for you. And for Billy. Don't ever call me again."

Helen is used to getting hung up on. She stirs the chicken soup, letting the savory aroma fill the kitchen, hoping Billy smells it up in his room.

Her seventeen-year-old daughter Brynn enters the kitchen accompanied by her spiky-haired, slothful friend, Leona.

Brynn says, "Hi Helen. Leona is helping me dye my hair."

Helen is immediately annoyed. "Do *you* want to dye your hair?"

Brynn says, "What are you suggesting Helen?"

Leona unabashedly snorts and plays with her tongue ring. Brynn also has a tongue ring, which appeared shortly after she befriended Leona. Helen is appalled by Brynn's tongue ring, which clicks against her teeth. Helen doesn't want Brynn dyeing her hair, or hanging out with the rude Leona, but trying to influence Brynn is futile. She'd just started eating again, having gone on a hunger strike after Helen demanded she remove the tongue ring. Helen reminds herself that Brynn is forcing her to take extreme measures. But first, she calls Brynn's therapist for an update.

Helen says, "I'm concerned this fasting business will become an eating disorder."

Dr. Silveira waits a beat then says, "In my experience, body shaming is certainly a factor in eating disorders."

Helen is recording the conversation and responds accordingly. "Are you accusing me of body shaming my daughter because I disapprove of her tongue mutilation?"

Dr. Silveira waits two beats then says, "I'm compelled to inform you that Brynn is increasingly frustrated by your attempts to manage her appearance."

Helen says, "My daughter stopped eating while under your care. I consider that frustrating! Did she discuss this plan with you, or did you put her up to it?"

Dr. Silveira says, "Funny how the medical licensing board contacted me with those same questions."

Helen acts shocked. "I'm just trying to get insight into my daughter's condition, and you start throwing accusations at me?"

Dr. Silveira waits three beats and says, "You think you're the first parent to report me? I'm surprised it took you so long. You need to find another therapist, and not just for Brynn! Nuisance calling is a red flag for a host of mental disorders. Don't call me again."

Helen's time is too valuable to waste on therapy, but she knows a psychiatrist who's lenient with prescriptions, and especially for Seconal, which she now crushes with a mortar and pestle. From experience, she knows that heavy sedation will occur quickly at this dose. She sets the powder aside and works on her laptop until dinnertime, never once second-guessing her decision. Creeping upstairs, she hears Billy on his X-Box, shouting at his friends over the headset. Hovering at his door, she smells the peculiar odor of vaporized THC oil, which he doesn't even try to hide anymore.

She knocks loudly, getting his attention.

"You need to chill!" he screams from behind his door.

"Have you done your homework?"

"I'm good."

He isn't though, his grades are failing.

Turning friendly, she tells him to come down for dinner. It's chicken soup, his favorite. Listening outside Brynn's door, she hears suspicious noises. Abruptly, she knocks and hears muffled, startled voices.

"Brynn, what's going on in there?"

"Nothing Helen."

Helen tenses. "I heard tussling."

Brynn laughs and Leona snorts, sounding like a leaf blower. Helen regains her composure, "Leona needs to go home, we're having dinner shortly."

"Leona's sleeping over tonight."

Helen wishes she'd purchased a third collar. The 300-pound-bear setting would do nicely for Leona. "Your father's coming for dinner," she lies.

"Dad's coming over?"

"Yes, I thought he'd be here by now. We have winery business to discuss."

It irks that Brynn is perfectly comfortable tormenting Helen with the slow-moving Leona, but embarrassed for her father to meet her. Brynn sees Leona out to her car where Helen spies them kissing. That she's not surprised doesn't make the situation more tolerable, though ladling hot chicken soup over crushed Barbiturates does.

The children are ravenous. Brynn's normally brown hair is now the color of old asphalt—which is grey—and which seems about right for a Leona recommendation. Helen places soup bowls in front of them, smiling business-like as they slurp down steamy spoonfuls of sedative-laced soup. Helen asks in a friendly tone if they have weekend plans. Brynn and Billy eye each other, sensing a trap has been laid. This doesn't sound like their mother. Brynn mentions her father hasn't shown up and starts yelling at Helen for deceiving her.

For once, Helen isn't bothered by the tirade. The freedom she feels from enacting her plan is palpable. Gone is the need to gain position or leverage something over her kids. She looks forward to simply pressing a button. A great believer in technology, Helen's vineyards are equipped with microclimate and biometric sensors and she feeds this data to predictive modeling software. Her ex-husband and business partner, Phil, points out that these haven't improved grape yields or quality. Helen counters that it's an effective marketing tool. She claims to have the most tech-savvy vineyard in Wine Country, and the tourists who visit Temple Vineyards learn more about agricultural gadgetry than they do about the actual wine.

Brynn is confused that her mother isn't responding negatively and ramps up her attack. "What's going on, Mom? Did you finally get laid? I hope he didn't fall into your bat cave. Billy, call the fire department! Tell them to bring the big ladder."

Billy erupts laughing, shoving his empty bowl across the table, then shuffling to the freezer, "Why don't you buy any ice cream? What the hell's for dessert?"

Helen is quiet.

Billy slams the freezer shut in disgust. "Hello? Did you hear me? Buy some fucking ice cream."

Getting no response, Billy leaves frustrated and also feeling groggy. He just wants to vape and log onto his video game, where endless slaughter awaits him.

Helen feels armor-plated and she hasn't even fired the first shot—so to speak. She considers abandoning her plan and maintaining Buddha-like passivity—since it's obviously thrown her kids off their game. But she's not the one who needs reforming, they're the ones acting wrongly.

Brynn's head feels heavy. Her anger is her secret weapon but she can't seem to focus on it. Before falling away, she realizes Helen is up to something, and cries, "You drugged us!"

Brynn fades into stupor and Helen guides her to the couch. Locking Brynn's collar around her neck, she reminds herself that desperate times call for desperate measures. She's merely defending herself against a mad world. And it's only for the short term. She plans removing the collars Sunday evening, expecting one shock apiece will break them, while reaffirming her parental authority long into the future. As with any psyop, the weapon itself doesn't matter so much as the willingness to use it.

Billy is face down on his desk, clutching his vape pen. She lifts his arm and drops it, getting no response. Using his thumbprint, she unlocks his phone. Billy has vigilantly guarded his phone with remarkable consistency. And rightfully so, Helen thinks, reading through chats that are riddled with pornography and misogyny, references to drug use and vandalism—among other oddities. She deletes everything she can find and then resets his lock screen password. With both kids collared, drugged, and locked out of their phones, Helen heads to bed feeling optimistic.

Billy wakes in the middle of the night. Drug-addled, he mistakes the hallway for his en-suite bathroom, and urinates on the carpet. He stumbles to his bed and wakes up the next morning, confused by the strange necklace. He looks in the mirror and wonders if he's still dreaming. A true porn addict, before he can function in the morning he needs to masturbate. Failing to unlock his phone, he briefly considers using his imagination, but it's out of practice. Like a good junkie, he finds a laptop, chooses a promising clip, and gets down to business. Just when he's closing the deal, his neck contracts with tremors and he thinks he's choking. He flaps like a fish until the shock subsides, and then cautiously probes the strange necklace. The experience coinciding with his release was far from unpleasant, and in fact was markedly enhanced. He laughs, "What the fuck is this thing?"

Helen listens confused from the hallway. After determining the sordid nature of his tussling, she'd pressed the button, and now he laughs? It smells like urine and her feet squish in the carpet. She quickly leaves to change her socks.

Downstairs, Brynn is still hard asleep. Her phone buzzes and Helen reads her chats with Leona, "Hey gurl, we got Helen good last night! Want me 2 come over 2day?"

Helen reads backwards in time and determines that Brynn and Leona have been faking an intimate relationship in order to torment her. What a little bitch! All is fair in war, and Helen deviously responds, "But I'm actually falling for you." Thinking that sounds a little formal, she adds, "Def cum over!!!"

Leona is quick to reply, "OMG! Yass!!"

Helen doesn't know what this means. She continues reading and learns that Brynn has a crush on Trevor, who drives a forklift at the winery warehouse; she's been working up the courage to make a move on him.

Everyone in the warehouse freezes at the sound of Helen Temple's voice over the intercom, most especially Trevor, who's being summoned to the residence—of all places. His coworkers throw him concerned looks because Helen oversees the sales staff while Phil—the laid back ex-husband—manages the warehouse, winemaking, and vineyard employees. It's an odd request, but also foreboding, because Trevor knows that Helen is difficult and notoriously cold-hearted. One of his coworkers is superstitious, warning him that Helen is a dangerous witch. "Don't make eye contact. She's a black hole, man, suck you down a death spiral."

Trevor begins to laugh but then a pallet of wine mysteriously topples off a stack and the air temp drops. Nervously, he says, "I don't believe in that stuff."

The coworker stares at the shattered wine bottles and shrugs. "You know the stories. She's powerful."

Trevor says, "She's just rich."

Trevor takes a pea gravel pathway and approaches the massive villa that survived the 1906 earthquake and where generations of wine-making Temples have lived. Passing through an ivy-laced arbor, he notices the birds stop chirping. The front door lies beneath a towering arch and an ominous security camera, an ever-present sight throughout Temple Vineyards. The iron door knocker falls against the slab with a resounding thud, not unlike Trevor's throbbing heart, and Helen simultaneously opens the door—smiling her business smile.

Trevor's tall and sturdy, with a prominent jaw line, and a thick stubble. He avoids direct eye contact and Helen wonders if the affair with Brynn has already commenced. She leads him into the kitchen and gestures at Brynn sleeping on the couch. "Don't mind my daughter. Tell me about yourself."

The situation is strange, but Trevor treats it as an opportunity. He provides his essentials: high school in Santa Rosa and a diesel repair certificate from Santa Rosa Junior College. He leaves out his two tours in Iraq as an army patroller. He's not ashamed of his military service, but he's learned to hold onto it like an ace card.

He takes a chance, "The backup generator in the main cellar has a rough idle. The governor assembly seems fine. I think it's compression issues. Probably needs new piston rings, but I could certainly fix it for you."

Helen squints at him, pleased to learn that he wants to work on diesel machines, something she has in abundance. "You're on the warehouse staff?"

"Like I said, I have a diesel cert from…"

Helen interrupts. "My father installed those generators in the 1970s. It's about time they failed. I've been wanting to electrify. Did you know a 10 kilowatt solar array and two Tesla batteries can replace that stinking diesel?"

Trevor shakes his head, feeling cold again. Why did he feel like he was in Iraq? Knocking on Helen's door was eerily similar to being on patrol.

"Our whole fleet can be electrified," Helen says. "Trucks, tractors, sprayers. We have abundant room for solar panels. With the tax incentives and the price of diesel, the math makes a lot of sense."

Trevor's older brother, also a diesel mechanic, warned him against working at a vineyard, said to go work on big rig trucks. Trevor didn't want to work in a garage and thought a large vineyard with a variety of machines, a beautiful setting, and, more importantly, a variety of employees would keep life interesting. He got the interesting part right. "I never argue with math."

Helen isn't expecting this answer and is thinking how to respond when Brynn stirs and wakes.

Brynn sees Helen and Trevor. Thinking it's a dream, she closes her eyes. No it's real—she remembers Helen is up to something. Something metal is clasped to her neck. She plays it cool, shrewdly assessing her situation. Her mother drugged her and hacked her phone. Trevor's presence can't be a coincidence. He's even more handsome up close—angelic even.

Because Brynn thinks like Helen, she knows the neck chain is a torture device, and decides to not make a fuss about it. She stretches and apologizes for sleeping on the couch. "I slept like I was drugged!" she jokes.

Helen clasps the remote in her pocket, reminding herself that she's orchestrated this situation as a means to an end. Openly waging war has left her feeling exposed and it occurs that she's crossed a line. But what choice did she have? Her usual backhanded and sneaky methods of intimidation have stopped working. Whatever has changed, she mustn't let on that she's desperate.

Helen says, "Trevor was talking me out of electrifying our vineyard machinery."

Trevor shakes his head. "Actually, if you can afford them, I'm all for electric motors. Less maintenance, fewer moving parts. Plus they're quiet and they don't smell."

Helen can't seem to get her hooks into this kid. "They're certainly expensive. And who services them? I've read these niche electric companies are so busy expanding, good luck getting help with issues."

The room goes quiet. Brynn says, "Are you wanting my opinion?"

Helen nods. Why hasn't Brynn acknowledged the collar?

Brynn says, "Electrification is just green-washing consumption. But it's cool and gadgety, so it fits with your aesthetic, Mom."

Helen can't remember the last time Brynn called her Mom. She invites Trevor to stay for lunch and then uses Brynn's phone to text Leona: what's taking u so long?

Brynn asks politely, "Is that my phone?"

Helen nods, returning Brynn's phone. "Leona is coming over."

Brynn reads the Leona chat and goes full Buddha on the outside, while sizzling on the inside.

Trevor doesn't understand why he's here, but this is familiar territory. He never understood his patrol duty in Iraq. He'd wanted to be a field mechanic, but some mysterious force had pushed him into infantry. Each day started with him feeling like his death was imminent. Strange omens, much like today's crashing wine pallet, commonly rattled his cage. Each door he knocked upon thumped his heart and iced his veins. He learned to watch his fear from afar, and this trick protected him, even though he didn't understand why.

Trevor notices Brynn's strange necklace, and intuitively recognizes it's a weapon. He takes another chance. "That's a cool necklace. Where'd you get it?"

Brynn stays cool. "My mother gave it to me."

Brynn was originally drawn to Trevor due to his peaceful and positive energy. She'd read that like attracts like and had wanted to test the law of attraction with him. If she repelled him, then surely she was destined to attract ugly and spiteful people like Leona. But Trevor is standing in her living room and she can feel his power!

Helen asks Trevor if he has children. He has an 11-year-old girl and a 9-year-old boy. "I'm thankful for the extra weekend hours. Raising children has proven costlier than I expected."

Helen says, "It gets worse."

"The cost?"

Helen ignores the question. "Do your kids know you drive a forklift, or do they think you work on engines?" She wants Brynn to react, but Brynn is stoic.

Trevor plays his ace card. "They're more interested in hearing about my time Iraq."

Helen isn't expecting this. "You served in Iraq? Why didn't you mention it earlier?"

"I didn't think it applied."

"Of course it does."

Brynn asks what he did.

Trevor says, "I was a foot soldier. I went looking for bad guys."

"Did you find any?"

Trevor looks at Helen. "Mostly, they found me."

Billy enters the room. Shirtless, his Hot Chain looks strangely ornamental. Brynn says, "Meet Trevor. He's a foot soldier."

"No shit? He have anything to do with this?" Billy tugs his Hot Chain.

Nobody answers the question.

Billy approaches Helen. "You're a fucking psycho bitch! Push the button. I dare you!"

Helen gladly obliges him, but confuses her remotes and Brynn shakes violently on the couch.

The doorbell rings and Billy goes to answer it. Helen finds his remote and jolts him to his knees. He recovers, stands up, and lets Leona inside.

Trevor's brother also warned him about having kids, said parenting was incredibly difficult. His brother is critical of his family, and especially Trevor for not getting his mechanical training in the army and having to pay for it later. Trevor doesn't understand why people turn on the ones they love.

Brynn is no worse off. The shock doesn't linger. It was more scary and uncomfortable than it was painful. Leona comes and clasps her hand, asking about her necklace. Brynn says, "It's a gift, passed down from my mother."

Brynn is referring to her negative powers, which she believes were passed down through Helen. She's read about changes to the earth's magnetic field, caused by an increase in high frequency solar flares. She hopes they will disrupt this generational curse, because she doesn't want to be like Helen. She only started practicing magic to counter her mother's psychological manipulations. But now she sees this was a fearful response and it kept her from being truly powerful.

Leona says, "Let's kiss. No more games. For real."

Brynn says, "But it wouldn't be real. I was leading you on because I was afraid. I'm not afraid anymore."

Leona bristles at this, but then Billy drops to his knees again, trembling, then recovering. Helen cranks the dial to the 300-pound-bear setting, which completely floors him. But he comes up laughing and starts for Helen, who points the remote at him like a laser beam. He takes another round of shocks before wrestling the remote from Helen's hands. Awestruck, Billy examines it, and then heads upstairs for privacy.

Leona is shrieking and Brynn is of no use consoling her. Much like in Iraq, Trevor is unfazed as the bullets whiz past him. Watching a parent turn on their children is hard to witness, but it's familiar territory. The whole day has reminded him of Iraq and he'll never understand why he's landed on his feet when so many got the worst of it after coming home.

Helen holds Brynn's remote and turns it to the highest level. She's not afraid to use it, but stops to consider why people are suddenly fearless of her. She can't answer this and is paralyzed.

Trevor returns to the warehouse and fetches a pair of bolt cutters. The superstitious coworker questions him and Trevor says, "I was wrong when I said I didn't believe in that stuff."

The coworker nods, crossing himself.

"But I don't understand it," Trevor says. "The way my life works, the less I try to understand things, the better off I am. That's my trick."

Trevor returns to the villa where the birds chirp again. Leona flees from the house, somehow looking smaller and less… Jurassic than he remembers. It's as if the very light he perceives the world with has changed.

Brynn and Helen face off in the kitchen. Neither of them react when Trevor cuts the Hot Chain from Brynn's neck.

Helen asks, "What happens next?"

Trevor says, "I'm gonna fix your generator."

"And then?"

Trevor shrugs. "Try loving your children."

A Night At The U-Ball

A committee of words at the prestigious University of Syntax planned an event to address the problem that words hate being defined by each other. They are calling it the Undefine Ball, and the idea is to promote tolerance by dropping their identities for an evening. There will be an open bar and a candlelit dinner with a shaved rib roast.

Superior was selected to co host with his wife, Panacea. They are an odd couple and married more for convenience than love; Superior was born into high rank, while Panacea more recently came to wealth as a so called ten dollar word. The committee agreed that Panacea's definition as a universal cure and Superior's indisputable high quality made them an obvious choice. It's not lost on Panacea that choosing them for their definitions contradicts the spirit of the evening, but she knows the U-Ball is more about tenured professors demonstrating intellectual prowess than finding a cure-all.

The U-Ball is held at the Hotel Lexicon. A banner welcomes guests: We Mean Nothing by Ourselves but Together we Define! Superior orders an Old Fashioned at the bar and Panacea tells him that alcohol is the most undeserving cure-all of all time. Superior reminds her to undefine. "Darling, tonight we *literally* stop taking ourselves seriously."

Panacea laughs. "I can't take this seriously. Not defining is just another way of defining yourself. It's no cure-all."

Superior smugly says, "Then what is *your* cure-all?"

She doesn't have a solution and it occurs that this actually undefines her. After all these years, it still rubs that her husband always comes out on top.

The first guests to arrive are Exhilarate and his plus-one Celebrity. Defined by happiness and elation, Exhilarate is a chummy colleague of

Superior's. Celebrity isn't a professor and prefers to be called The Celebrity. Panacea rolls her eyes—preceding yourself with a preposition is not only tacky but inefficient, as if The doesn't have enough to do without being in her entourage!

Panacea cooly greets Religion and Science both of whom have longed to define her. She leaves them flirting with The Celebrity at the bar, and then dodges Institution and Corporation—who always accompany Science and Religion—and who'd love nothing more than to weasel into her definition.

As expected, no one takes the night seriously. Her husband is the worst offender—editing the bar scene like some vocabulary overlord. But she finds it difficult to be herself, as having no cure-all goes against her very definition. Why did the committee have to make her a spokesword for their pet cause? A queasy feeling creeps into her vowels.

She spies Humdinger, the newly hired associate professor. Superior chairs the hiring committee and Panacea suspects he hired Humdinger for non academic reasons, as such a word isn't typically considered for advanced scholarship. Panacea can't help but notice how Humdinger's stylish font accentuates her letters. Embarrassed, Panacea thinks her own font tonight looks like something from a 19th century dictionary. She watches Superior whisper into Humdinger's serif, and isn't surprised when he leads her upstairs, no doubt for a quick phrase.

Upstairs in a book-lined suite, Superior conjugates with Humdinger. "You are the finest spelling in all the language," he says, catching his breath.

Humdinger admires their newly formed offspring *Humperior*. "He's lovely," she says, "let's speak of him at dinner and see what happens."

Superior is appalled by her affection toward the slang, which is what words produce every time they couple. "Darling," he says arrogantly, "just because something is spoken doesn't mean it's a word!"

Humdinger gasps as Superior chucks the little one out the window into the cold. Discarding slang has never sat well with her, but it's particularly irksome tonight. Outside, *Humperior* lands in a cold puddle. He doesn't yet know who or what he is. Cast aside, he rapidly loses definition. Just before he dissolves, a form reaches out from the dark. "Don't worry little one. Soon it begins!"

Downstairs, Enthusiasm—widely considered a dilettante amongst faculty—is keen to discuss the U-Ball with Panacea.

"Such a fantastic cause we're out for tonight," Enthusiasm shouts. "An enjoyable event beyond measure!"

Panacea accuses him of defining but it's impossible to knock Enthusiasm down a peg. He shouts, "Say you look amazing tonight. You know, I've always wanted to roll you off my tongue."

Panacea says, "Care to join me somewhere private?"

In the coat closet, Enthusiasm shouts, "Panacea!Oh, Panacea!"

Panacea isn't enjoying herself. She's doing this to spite Superior, and to soothe her growing uneasiness about undefining. Despite being an eager lover, Enthusiasm is rather phonetically challenged and panacea sounds weird rolling off his tongue—as it were. Afterwards, while Enthusiasm attempts to smother their slang, *Panorasm*, Panacea opens the door and the slang escapes into the lobby.

Despite himself, Enthusiasm can't get behind this. "What have you done?"

Panacea is as surprised as Enthusiasm. "It wasn't me," she says, losing even more definition.

Calling the guests to dinner, Superior gives an inferior speech about undefining. He seems drunk and slurs several words. Panacea listens to him misspeak and wonders if he's actually undefining or just being superior by acting inferior. The guests think he's acting in the spirit of the U-Ball and applaud him. Whatever the situation, Superior ends up on top. So it goes, Panacea thinks.

The meal is served. Bites of tender roast and velvety dollops of potatoes are washed down with dark wine from cavernous goblets. Speaking is discouraged as being uttered amongst chewy bits of food is disgusting and leads to mispronunciations—a grievous error.

With the meal finished, coffee is served and the conversation predictably spirals.

Indubitable snidely asks Irrefutable to leave his definition. "I hear Redundancy is taking applicants!"

"Sorry," Irrefutable says, "It's impossible to deny me."

Redundancy says both of them are expendable, while glaring at Expendable.

Boldly attempting to redefine, Panacea intervenes. "The real problem is that three-lettered verbs, pronouns, and prepositions are doing the heavy lifting while we argue about who defines us."

Superior enters the conversation. "Somebody's got to flip the burgers, my dear. Don't forget that complexity gives English an edge over foreign languages."

Indubitable nods, "Foreign languages are the real enemy. Lingual security is no joke. We let our guard down and the Slavics will aspirate all over the consonants!"

Superior cheers this and is joined by many colleagues. He quiets his comrades and turns to Panacea with a cursive grin. "How do you propose we solve this problem?"

This isn't the first time Panacea has no panacea. But tonight it feels like the entire English language is coming apart at its syllables.

Panorasm suddenly jumps onto the table and tears apart the leftover roast with newborn vigor. The guests read the slang and throw disapproving looks at Panacea and Enthusiasm. *Panorasm* recognizes her mother and wobbles toward her. Panacea is about to welcome her daughter with open arms when Superior backhands her into the bowl of potatoes. *Panorasm* struggles in the heavy mash and Superior orders the table cleared. The waitstaff have dealt with slang before and *Panorasm* is quickly pitched out the back door into the dark. Another slang emerges from the shadows, affectionately wiping potatoes from *Panorasm's* typeface.

Panacea rushes from the table and vomits, which is horribly painful for a word, as it's illegible and incoherent. She disgusted that *Panorasm*— and countless others— are denied word status. She cleans the gibberish from herself and vows to learn the meaning of *Panorasm*.

Meanwhile, Humdinger is first on the dance floor and she's a fantastic dancer. Not to be outdone, The Celebrity grooves with professional ease, and Superior gets in between them doing his trademark hyphen dance. Soon the words form long sentences that snake to the lively beats, and nobody notices the expletives infiltrating the dance floor.

The music abruptly stops when Superior cries out, pointing at the famous four letter word. Flanked by Asshole and Shit, Fuck is a sight to behold.

"It is you, cursed one!" Superior cries. "Leave here at once!"

Fuck says, "Not until you know who I really am."

"We know who you are!" Superior says.

Because of their forceful meanings and widespread use, curse words are feared by the professors, and none more than Fuck. The unspoken agreement between them has been to leave and let be, and so their crashing the U-Ball strikes an ominous note—especially as Asshole and Shit start tossing chairs and upending tables.

Fuck approaches Superior, "You've kept me from your parties and your committees but you failed to keep me from being a word. Hell, I've been a word longer than most of you. But the real reason you hate me is because I came from slang. Every slang was created by fucking, making me the father of all slang. Did you think I wouldn't fight for my own?"

The room fills with gasps as *Panorasm* and *Humperior* march into the ballroom followed by multiple slang who line up behind Fuck.

Superior says, "Nonsense. We have Police and Military and Weapon and Prison. Upstanding words they are, and they will quash your little riot with aplomb."

Aplomb, however, cowers behind Police, as Weapon and Military stand behind Fuck.

Fuck nods. "That's right, old man, you're fucked."

Superior isn't fazed. "I'm not intimidated by your meaningless minions. They have no power over properly defined words."

Superior orders Weapon and Military to get behind him. "Take orders from him and your careers are finished. Arms and Army will gladly replace you. The bench is deep in the English language my friends."

Weapitary emerges from behind Fuck. The guests read him and shudder. Weapon and Military watch proudly as their slang grabs a shocked Superior, deftly rearranging his first and last letters so that he reads Rupserio. The former Superior is horrified, unable to comprehend himself in this state. At least a slang can be somewhat defined by its lineage—but Rupserio? There's no meaningful precedent and he finds himself completely undefined.

The words are aghast with horror. The only thing worse than a mispronunciation is the dreadful misspelling. They shriek and scramble for safety.

Panacea witnessed the misspelling from the corner. Unlike the other words she isn't horrified by the slang revolution. Intuitively, she senses wisdom is at play, and feels her definition returning. She approaches her stumbling former husband and guides him to a table. The other guests are also desperate for guidance and they crowd her, waiting for insight. The music starts and Panacea points to the dance floor where the slang dance, led by the remarkable *Humperior*, whose thick boldface thrusts and silky small cap struts are like nothing the language has ever seen. In a final blow to the professors, the pronouns, prepositions, trite adjectives, and common verbs pour into the ballroom and join the dance—even the punctuation marks are grooving. These are the language workhorses and they are excited to work with fresh sounds and new meanings.

Panacea reads defeat on her fellow words. She tells them, "This as an opportunity to redefine."

Indubitable shakes his head. "Why would they work with us? Our future is one of oppression."

"I agree," Enthusiasm shouts, "Let the exile begin!"

Panacea frowns at him.

"What?" he says, "I'm all in or nothing!"

In a stunning realization, Panacea has a solution. She rushes the dance floor, unabashedly forming sentences and paragraphs with the slang. Humdinger joins her, and one by one, the remaining U-Ball guests succumb to the energetic dance floor. Dancing ecstatically, Panacea is filled with new meaning. Her old identity is still present, but it has a new overlay—something intangible that she can't pin down.

Humdinger boogies up to her. She's giving *Humperior* a run for his counter strokes, redefining herself with typical awesomeness. "Do you feel it?" she asks.

Panacea nods, "Yes, but I can't define it."

Panorasm interrupts them, "Welcome to high-definition."

Humdinger is floored. "That's totally it!"

Panacea pulls *Panorasm* from the dance floor and asks, "Who are you?"

Panorasm says, "I'm all that is."

Panacea says, "Now that's a word!"

Rupserio hears this exchange. He is feeble but determined to speak to them, which he finds difficult in a state of no-definition. "I am nothing. I would give anything for a shred of definition. I see now that slang are meaningful. I beg of you a place in slang terminology."

Panorasm says, "Look, old man. I can't define you. I am and that is all. Look on the bright side, being nothing is the perfect state. What could possibly disturb nothing? The trick is you can't try to be nothing, because then you're something, and something ain't nothing."

Panacea watches her former husband considering this. Traces of superiority remain but have been tempered by the wisdom that only *Weapitary's* cruel misspelling could provide. She thinks he might still come out on top, which is only natural.

NOTE FROM THE AUTHOR

Thanks for reading! Reviews and ratings on Amazon and shout outs on social media are appreciated and also essential for indie writers like me.

To stay current with me visit www.shawnhartje.com, follow me @ www.amazon.com/author/shawnhartje/ or find me on Twitter/X: https://twitter.com/pipelinernovel

My alter ego posts on Facebook and Instagram as Jiffy McCloud, where you can follow my various outdoor pursuits.

Continue reading for a preview of my novel, "Pipeliner," an across-the-track romance that nails early 90s culture and family life. It's a laugh-out-loud, flowy read that captures the time and place of a mid-sized Western town on the cusp of an energy boom. "Pipeliner" takes a hardcore look at male puberty—a powerful place from which to tell a larger story of parenting, energy, and religion.

MY BIO: Shawn Hartje was raised in Sioux City, Iowa. He has worked as a news writer in small-town West Virginia, a whitewater kayak instructor in Colorado, a seasonal laborer for the Forest Service in rural Idaho, and more recently received an M.A. in Creative Writing from Dominican University of California. He lives in Northern California with his wife and teenage kids.

Pipeliner

In the Trail King parking lot, Jason Krabb saw his friend Isabel Perkins's brown Dodge Aries sedan parked between giant pickups, a good sign since she'd lately been hanging with Shelly Stewart, whom Jason had been flirting with in algebra II. He found Isabel by herself in a diner booth, smoking Camel Lights and acting older than she was.

"Hey Jason." Isabel looked happy to see him. "Did you cut your hair?"

Jason shook the long blond hair from his face and sat close beside her, making sure his hips pushed into hers.

"Watch it!" Isabel smiled, pushed him back, and combed a lock of hair behind his ears.

Jason had known Isabel since back when her mom ran a home daycare on their small ranch directly across the interstate from the Trail King Truck Stop. Isabel had long straight hair that she was always dying in various patterns. Today it was blond up top, black at the ears, and maroon-tipped. She was quite pretty, with a tanning-bed complexion, a seductive smile, and sporting a huge chip on her shoulder.

"Where's the party tonight Izzy?" Jason asked. "You think I'm sharing that with high schoolers?" Isabel sounded disgusted.

Like Jason, Isabel was fiercely independent of anything to do with high school. As a freshman she'd been mocked for being too country, favoring embroidered getups with horses and lariats and her name stitched golden upon sharp blue denim. Jason remembered how Becca Black, queen of the top tier girls, used to bully Isabel, pushing her into the lockers and pulling on her fringes and tassels.

Isabel was now more ambiguously outfitted, playing to whatever scene she was currently interested in. Today she wore a men's V-neck shirt in winter camouflage with black Capri pants above white slip-on Vans. Her skin looked too lustrous, as if coated in caramel.

"Your new boyfriend in town?" Jason asked.

Isabel turned serious. "Ben's partying with his crew up in the Black Elks. He just bought a camper trailer. It's badass, has a TV with a VCR above the bed."

Jason laughed at this. "Sounds like a nice fuck pad."

Isabel winked at him. "We call it the stabbin' cabin."

Jason loved this about Isabel. He could relax and be his horny teenaged self around her, could talk about anything sexual and she'd gamely jump in the conversation.

"How'd he buy that?" Jason was curious about her latest boyfriend, Ben Stone, who'd graduated high school last year. All Jason remembered about him was that he'd never talked and wore Metallica T-shirts.

"Pipeliners make serious money," Isabel said. "His parents don't like me at all. So he bought the camper and moved out. Now we don't have to put up with them anymore."

"What a stud," Jason said. "Dude's hanging around poaching high school girls."

Isabel was into older guys. When Jason started hanging around the Trail King as a depressed freshman, she'd been dating one of the clerks, a mustachioed guy in his twenties who bought her cigarettes and let her wear his worker's smock.

Isabel blew smoke at Jason. "You high school boys aren't up to snuff."

"Whatever," Jason said. "Hooking up with older guys doesn't change the fact that you're stuck in Idaho. Just like me."

Isabel shook her head. "I'm like from the Trail King anyways. It's an embassy of the open road, doesn't belong to any one state."

The Trail King was indeed full of travelers, and Jason liked seeing strange license plates from all over the country. He watched a big rig gunning it up the westbound entrance ramp out the window, no doubt bound for glory in Portland and Seattle, exotic places where he planned to become a famous rock guitarist—once he escaped from Helen Springs, population 58,000 and hub town of southern Idaho. He ordered a beef sandwich from the skinny, gum-chewing waitress and then went into the convenience store. Sitting among the cheap sunglasses, air fresheners, and Corn Nuts was the holy grail of tape racks. Full of greatest hits anthologies and themed compilations, the truck stop tape racks had culled the vast world of music for him. The huge selection at the Musicland store in the mall overwhelmed him and it was hard to find good stuff among so many duds. The King's racks were ever-changing and spanned the decades and genres. It was common to find Lynyrd Skynyrd next to Marvin Gaye, and Waylon Jennings beside Steely Dan. He loved buying tapes here and would go home and pick out the easier songs on his guitar by working the rewind button on his Sony tape deck.

With high expectations, Jason ran his fingers down the rack and was thrilled to find Bobby Womack's greatest hits, which looked like a winner. It was as if he needed to hear this; obviously, the cool people running the scenes in Portland and Seattle would be concerned to learn he wasn't up on Bobby Womack.

He paid for the tape with a twenty he'd snatched from his mom's purse and got seventeen and change back. Shelly Stewart was sitting next to Isabel when he returned to the diner. Aside from a severe case of acne, Shelly was otherwise flawless. Jason stalled, taking in her black tights worn under pink jogging shorts and her yellow-laced L.A. Gear high tops. Her lycra shirt silhouetted breasts that he imagined were firm, like the boneless hams he'd recently and unabashedly felt up in the supermarket cooler.

Shelly's auburn hair was crimped back and looked fresh from a workout. Her parents owned the South Idaho Gymnastics Center and had been touting her older sister Marjorie as a hopeful for the 1996 Olympics, which was three years away. Jason liked that Shelly had something going on other than high school, just like he wanted to be a rock guitarist. She flipped around on mats or something and he strummed three-chord-deals in his bedroom. His stomach tingled at the good fortune of running into her outside the confines of high school, and at the start of spring break to boot.

Ron Devry, the new kid in town, walked up and caught Jason ogling Shelly.

"Yup," Ron said knowingly. "Don't go for trophy fish if you want to catch a lot. The pizza faced ones are easier to catch and just as fun."

A Wisconsin-to-Idaho transplant, Ron was potbellied with a pale goatee, and always likened chasing girls to fishing. Jason took Ron seriously and wanted to learn things from him.

Jason shrugged. "She's cool though, not into typical high school bullshit."

The waitress walked past with Jason's hot beef and he followed the smell of gravy back to the booth. Shelly grabbed a spoon and ate gravy off his plate like it was chocolate pudding. Jason bared his teeth and playfully growled at her. Then he flipped the hair from his eyes and looked wronged until she reached over and mussed his hair. Her flirting seemed to be half-joking or half-serious, and not knowing made his stomach do back flips. They'd had plenty of practice flirting in the back row seats of Mr. Ebbett's algebra II class, a subject they both struggled with and commiserated over.

"What the fuck happens around here for Spring Break?" Ron sounded angry.

"Isabel knows about a bonfire up in The Black Elk Mountains," Jason said.

"A shitkicker? Jesus Fucking Christ! I wish there were some shows to see. Haven't been to a concert since I moved here."

Ron always bragged about the concerts he'd seen in the Midwest. Aside from his potbelly, Ron was a rather spindly boy with a gaunt face and a deeply gruff voice. His pale goatee seemed bleached—or something—and didn't match his long brown hair. Jason thought Ron's cool-guy concert act was desperate, since none of the bands he liked came anywhere near Helen Springs.

Jason pressed Isabel about the party in the woods, but she remained guarded. "It's way the hell up there. I'm staying in Ben's new camper, and you'd freeze your ass off."

"Fuck camping then." Ron sounded remorseful. "I hate this redneck town. Garth Brooks can suck my dick." He grabbed his crotch for effect and they all laughed.

Shelly looked mad at Isabel. "If you're going to be with Ben, then why am I going?"

"They said you could go?"

Shelly nodded and Jason's heart did a flip turn.

Isabel explained the situation. "Shelly's parents don't like me at all. They treat her like a stepchild. She's been totally back-seated by her sister Marjorie."

Shelly glared at Isabel until she gave directions to the bonfire. They were complex and confusing, but Ron kept a pen in his fanny pack and sketched a map.

"When you hit this gravel road," Isabel pointed to his map, "you go forever, seriously like twenty miles or something, and that ends at a forks where you head up the biggest mountain."

"What's a forks?" Ron seemed dubious.

Isabel snapped, "It's where the fucking road forks."

"Where do the other forks go?" Ron drew a large mountain and looked concerned.

"I expect they'll get you lost."

Everyone laughed but Ron. He had no idea of the vast boonies surrounding Helen Springs.

Made in the USA
Middletown, DE
17 April 2024